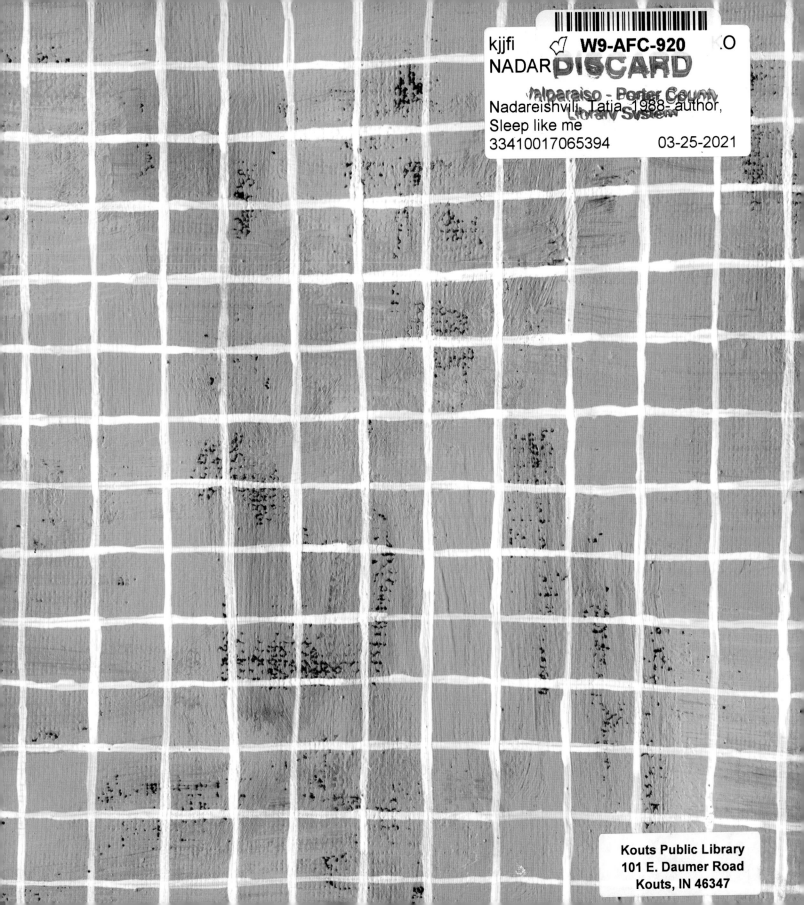

TATIA NADAREISHVILI studied illustration and graphic design at the Tbilisi State Academy of Arts. After working as an art therapist and teacher, she now works as an illustrator in her own studio. One day, while watching a random TV channel, Tatia came across a video of sperm whales sleeping upright in dark blue water. That inspired her to research the ways other animals sleep, which led to the creation of *Sleep Like Me*.

Tatia lives in Tbilisi, Georgia, in Eastern Europe. This is her first book published in the English language.

First published in the United States in 2021
by Eerdmans Books for Young Readers,
an imprint of Wm. B. Eerdmans Publishing Co.
Grand Rapids, Michigan

www.eerdmans.com/youngreaders

Original edition published in German under the title *Schlaf gut*
Copyright © 2017 by Baobab Books, Basel, Switzerland

English-language translation © Eerdmans Books for Young Readers 2021

Manufactured in China

29 28 27 26 25 24 23 22 21   1 2 3 4 5 6 7 8 9

ISBN 978-0-8028-5566-4

A catalog record of this book is available from the Library of Congress.

Illustrations created with acrylic and digital materials.

FSC
www.fsc.org

MIX
Paper from
responsible sources
FSC® C144853

Sleep Like Me

WRITTEN AND ILLUSTRATED BY
Tatia Nadareishvili

EERDMANS BOOKS FOR YOUNG READERS   GRAND RAPIDS, MICHIGAN

The little boy can't go to sleep.

"I guess I'll go for a walk."

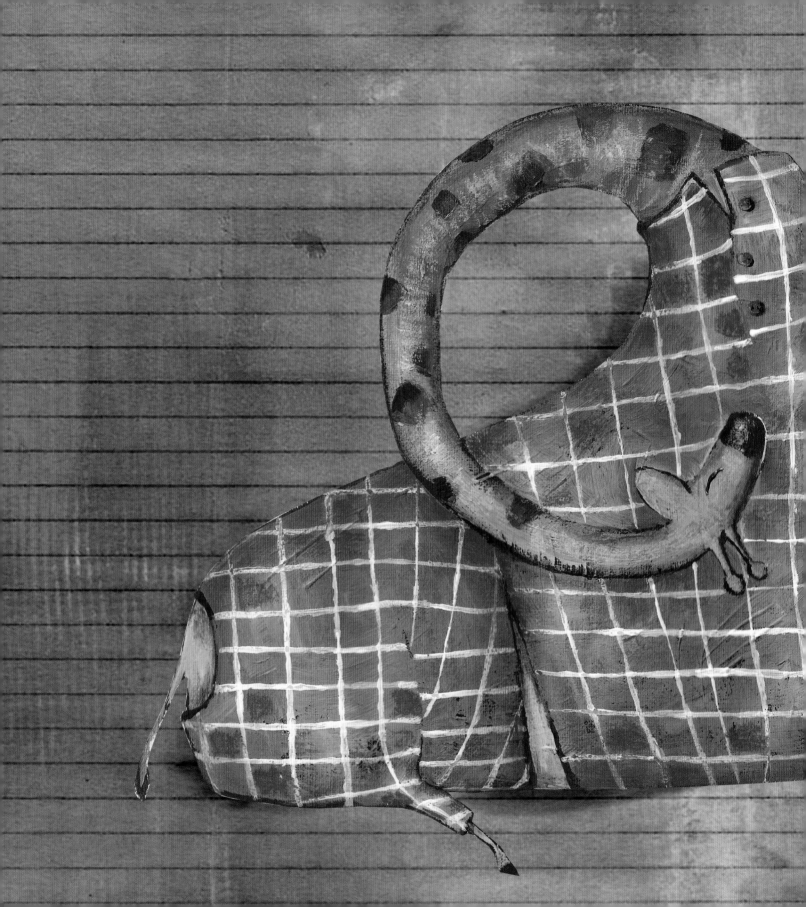

"I can't go to sleep," the boy says.

"Just rest your head on your back,
and then you'll nod off. That's how
I go to sleep," the giraffe says.

The boy tries, but doesn't
have any luck.

"No, not on your back! You have to tuck your head under your wing," says the bird.

The boy tries, but
it doesn't work.

"You know what? Just hang from the tree
with your hands and feet. That's how I go
to sleep," says the sloth, then shows the
boy how to do it.

The boy tries this too, with no success.

The otters tell him: "Let yourself float on your back, and you'll go to sleep. That's how we do it."

The boy tries floating on the water. But he still can't go to sleep.

"No, you can't just float! You have to dive deep into the water," the sperm whales say. "Then you'll fall asleep, just like we do."

The boy does as he is told. But this doesn't work either.

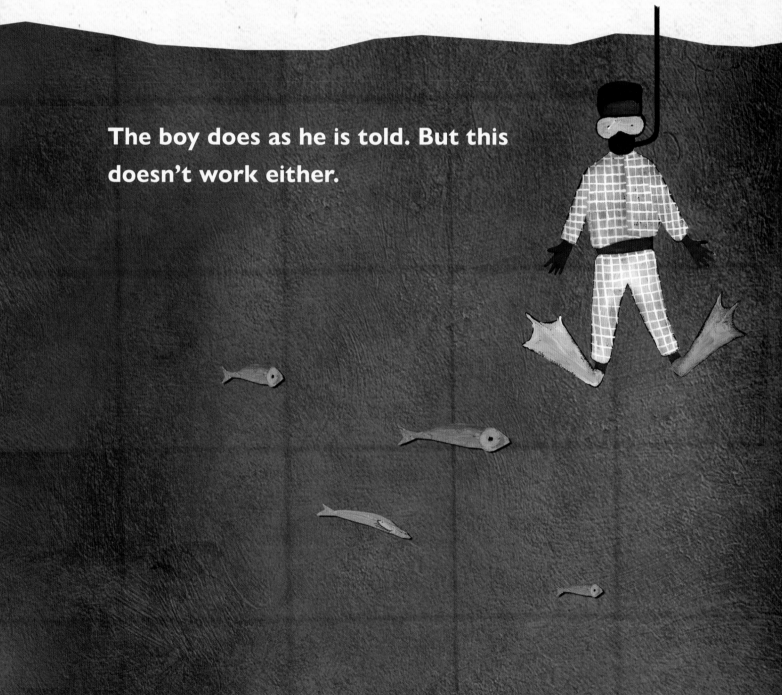

"Are you trying to sleep lying down?" the
horse asks. "If you want to go to sleep,
you need to be standing up, like me."

The boy stands still for
quite some time,
but he still isn't
tired enough
to sleep.

Then he notices the koalas.

"Come climb up the tree
and make yourself
comfortable in the fork
of a branch. Then you'll
go to sleep. That's how
we do it."

The boy climbs into the tree,
but he still can't fall asleep.

"You can't just sit in the branches—
you have to hang head-first from them,"
the bats recommend.

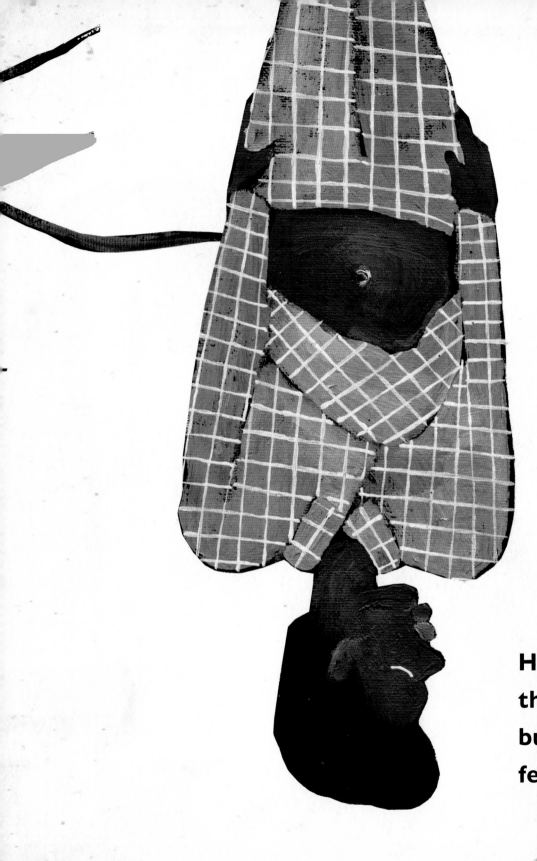

Head first
the boy hangs,
but he doesn't
feel sleepy at all.

He carries on with his walk and meets the ducks.

"Come and sleep with us. You just need to keep one eye open. That's how we sleep."

The boy joins the ducks, one eye closed.

It might work fine for them,
but he can't go to sleep.

"Hey, can you help me go to sleep?" he says to the albatross.

"Sure! Happy to help. But you can't sleep on the ground. You need to come up into the air. That's how I go to sleep."

But not even flying helps.

Meanwhile the boy is feeling a little tired.
"I'd better go home and rest."

Back in his room he climbs into bed.

After only a few minutes,
the boy is sound asleep.

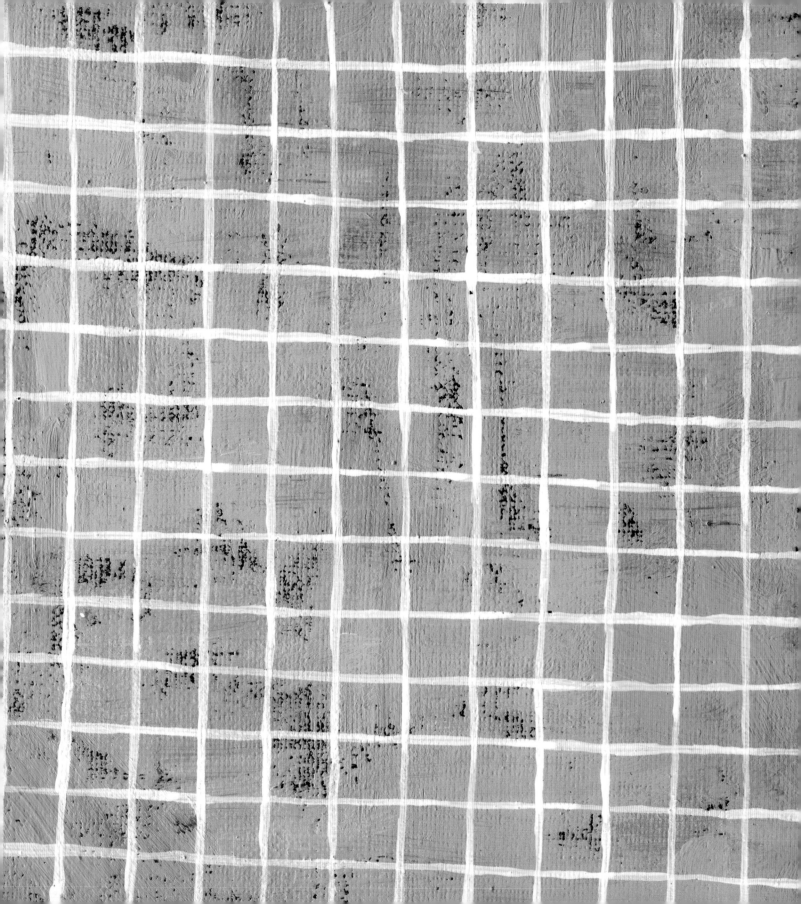